The Sower's Harvest

THE SOWER'S HARVEST

Carol Woolgar

SPIRITUAL WARFARE 4COVID19
How God is the same today, as He was yesterday and will be tomorrow

ReadersMagnet, LLC

What Others Are Saying

"Wow! This really makes you think how we as Christians have sabotaged our own destination, future, and well-being in this life by not putting all our faith and trust in Him the Almighty One."
- Teresa Kongable, Orlando, Florida

"You have laid your heart here before us and have invited us in. Your invitation has helped to create hope in our own hearts. Thanks for being transparent and willing to share your life's journey with those of us who may be afraid of the nest step. It all comes down to trust."
- Brenda Key, Winter Garden, Florida

"I believe Carol had a revelation from God that only can be felt when we have descended into a deep darkness and ascended to the grace of heaven's steps."
- Earlene DeGagne, Ocoee, Florida

2021
THE SOWER'S HARVEST
Spiritual Warfare 4COVID19

2008
THE SOWER'S TRUST
13 years prior…

THE SOWER'S HARVEST

Carol Woolgar

SPIRITUAL WARFARE 4COVID19

How God is the same today, as He was yesterday and will be tomorrow

The Sower's Harvest.
Copyright © 2022 by Carol Woolgar.

Published in the United States of America

| ISBN | Paperback: | 978-1-958030-94-3 |
| ISBN | eBook: | 978-1-958030-95-0 |

All rights reserved. No part of this publication may be reproduced, stored in a retrieval system or transmitted in any way by any means, electronic, mechanical, photocopy, recording or otherwise without the prior permission of the author except as provided by USA copyright law.

The opinions expressed by the author are not necessarily those of ReadersMagnet, LLC.

ReadersMagnet, LLC
10620 Treena Street, Suite 230 | San Diego, California, 92131 USA
1.619. 354. 2643 | www.readersmagnet.com

Book design copyright © 2022 by ReadersMagnet, LLC. All rights reserved.

Cover design by Ericka Obando
Interior design by Dorothy Lee

*We all have a path in life
which we build through
the choices we make.
Sometimes we stumble,
sometimes we fall,
but when God is
the light at our feet
guiding the path of our lives,
we fulfill a predestined plan,
that of...
The Spirit Walker*

- C. W.

*To my two wonderful boys,
Zachary Michel and Bradley Marshall.*

May God always guide you with His Spirit, and may your hearts and minds always be open for the winds of change.

Live in peace, prosper well, but most important, be reminded to sacrifice and always be ready to give!

I am waiting for you in spirit always.

I love you.

Mom
xoxo

****

*AND TO
A Wonderful Man Named Ed
'I was blessed to have you during this Special Season of my life!'
YCG, Always, Carol xoxox*

Acknowledgments in the Name of Love

I want to thank my Lord and Savior Jesus Christ, who paid the ultimate price for me. His mercy and grace are the two greatest gifts He continuously gives me daily.

To my parents, thank you for always loving me, even through the hardest times of your lives!

To my siblings, thank you for always caring and protecting me from harm's way and allowing me to rejoice in the love of our family—for that I am eternally grateful.

To my boys—Zachary, thank you for being wiser than your years. It has helped "guide" my life! Bradley, thank you for always making me laugh when I needed it most!

To my special friend, Debbie, for making a simple suggestion through the sending of an email that I share my story with others on "how" I got through this journey.

Finally to my Prince, my Knight, my Hero, my Husband, Robert {Bob} Keith Williams. Your passing in May 2020 may have left me without you, but our memories will last me my lifetime! I Love You Forever & Always Your Girl, C. xoxox

Contents

Pre-Preface xv
Preface xix

Part I
The First Book of Life: The Miracle Seed

Introduction 3
The Initial Miracle Request 6
Fulfillment of the Request 10
My Story BIBLE 16
The Seeds of Life 20
The Spirit Walker 24

Part II
The Second Book of Life: The Spirit Walker

Introduction 31
Prelude to Steps of the Spiritual Walker 33
Spoken Silence 36

Part III
Revelation of the Scrolls

Scroll 1: The Approach (Attitude) 42
From Surrendering to Stripped Away 43
I Am 45
Scroll 2: The Sacred Time (Trust) 46
It Isn't Easy to be Patient 49
Scroll 3: The Inheritance (Miracles) 51
On Powerful Prayer: The Miracle Inheritance 53

Scroll 4: The Stillness (Commitment) 59
Hear Me, See Me, Feel Me 61
Scroll 5: The Embrace (Faith) 66
Can You Imagine 67
Scroll 6: The Change Of Heart (Love) 70
Feeling Guilty—Almost but Not Quite! 71
Scroll 7: The Seed (Doing) 74
The Guiding Seed 75
God's Revelation to Me on Sowing 76
How to Sow 77
Finale 79
Big Decision, Baby Steps 80
Saying Yes to God 81
Wherever You May Be 82
THE SOWER'S TRUST 83

Pre-Preface

It is truly safe to say that **God Was, Is and will Always Be** *the same He was yesterday, today, and tomorrow. God will use your troubles and work things out...*THE MOST IMPORTANT THING YOU HAVE TO HANG ONTO AND REMEMBER FOREVER AND ALWAYS IS, *'TRUST IN HIS PERFECT TIMING'!!!*

Not yours, not when you think it should be, it is when He knows it needs to be done, taken care of, addressed, brought to full fruition...only then, if you have been obedient in **Trust to Him,** will He show you the way!

You will continue to fail; you will continue to fall... Just remember He will always be there to pick you up and show you the way. Time is on His side and when you have the true heart of a servant and seek His face, He willl never, ever leave nor forsake you!
Know at all times that He guides you, gently to those still waters...
Know at all times that He Loves you unconditionally...
Know at all times that He aches as you do, and He will see you through...

I wrote this book in 2008 initially, retitled it and added this Pre-Preface to tell you this...

God used what I imagined was a total and complete useless tool in my 'tool belt of life' back in 2008, to bless me with it today above and beyond what Satan had taken away from my family in the Real Estate Market Crash of 2008. Today I am on the flip side of my story, my life thirteen years ago, and am here to tell you firsthand that *God is Good, always!* That when we Trust Him, Believe and have Faith in Him, hang on to Him and do not let go…He is always there for us, always has been, always is and always will be.

In February 2008 I had to obtain a realtor license to work and put food on our table - I did not love what I was doing or how I was using it. It was not my fit; it just was not me. It did not last exceptionally long, and I almost came so remarkably close to not renewing it - but I did! I hung on to it for eight years not knowing why I was, and in 2015 God opened a door for me to use it again, and I have not looked back since.

Today, because the epidemic of COVID-19 has changed so much in our working world and the way we function, the real estate market has seen an unprecedented demand for housing as people work more from home.

You see God knew that, He knew, he saw, and already planned my path for this time. The only thing I had to do and am still doing, is Trusting Him for what lays ahead of me… my spiritual growth has allowed me to do so with unshakable confidence, with peace and joy in knowing that I already have victory!

We serve an almighty and powerful God! Do not let your circumstances today deter you from what His plans are for your tomorrow.

My hope, as I prepare for the re-printing of this book, is that it finds all of you that need His light during these perilous times - for all of you that have been affected by COVID-19. For those of you that have lost loved ones, homes, businesses, relationships, money, cars, and self-confidence.

Know this, know that this journey is exactly that - a journey especially designed for you. You are going to be stretched beyond what you think you can carry emotionally, but you will! Some days are going to feel like you are face down in the mud, and you might be spending a little more time on your knees than you may ever have - and that's ok too because know this ... it is there that God will meet you...it is there that He will change you, guide, love and support you. Let him be the potter and allow yourself to be clay. Allow yourself to be taken care of like a child - His child, because He is your Heavenly Father, and He loves you unconditionally no matter how much of a mess you might think you are in! It's OK! He is your healer, provider, and shelter when your life is falling apart so that pieces of your life can fall back into place, according to His pre-destined plan for you...that of the Spirit Walker!

Preface 2014

Please allow me to introduce myself. My name is Carol and I live in Central Florida. I have been blessed with two very special boys - Zachary, aged nineteen, and Bradley, aged seventeen.

I have long since wanted to put together
on paper what I thought were ideas and feelings
about things that I knew something about.
Well, I'm here to tell you first and foremost
that all great and wonderful things are a
combination of who you are and the
precious touch of God's almighty hand.

You see, for years now, I've accumulated more
Post-it notes, more handfuls of book beginnings
that I care to count. I have a file that is thicker
than I even *want* to scan through for the
"perfect" idea because I know the words being
written and the ideas that are flooding
my mind right now have been combined
to create my first book that God has been
helping me diligently prepare for many years now!

So I hope that you'll enjoy,
be touched by, and maybe even be moved
by what it is that I have to share.
I have long believed that writing a book
was something you had to create from
the outside in (based on your experiences),
but I have come to fully realize that books—great
books—are really written from the inside out.

PART I

THE FIRST BOOK OF LIFE: THE MIRACLE SEED

Introduction

*One Woman's Grace-Filled Journey
of Heavenly Triumphs over Worldly Defeats*

Regardless of your surroundings, what you're about to do next will reap in results from the fact that you've either consciously planted a seed into something or not. It is very challenging, I know, to continuously have the mind and the heart of a sower. Our daily lives are filled with nonstop schedules, events, and routines that demand so very much from each and every one of us. But let me assure you that when you rise up in the morning, knowing that every day you start with a fresh clean field (of life) that has been well prepared, you are being given an opportunity to create a new end to something that may have had a bad start.

I believe with all my heart and soul that the first preparation for your field of life starts with the purest motive, which is giving. Matthew 6:3 says, "Our motives for giving to God and to others must be pure." God has revealed to me that although my life has been filled with many opportunities to give, in which I have, my intentions were not always for His glory! I am here to tell you that it must be for His glory because no matter who knows what you are doing to give to others, it is God who knows the focus of your heart most when you are doing so.

My personal preparation for this book was for God to help me understand the first step and the importance on *how* to give. After searching my heart and spending time alone with God, I have realized the true reason He wanted me to grasp this meaning so clearly. And now that I have been enlightened and prepared through His World to receive this message, I know that He wanted to bring me clarity at this very particular time in my life because of the many trials and tribulations I had just lived through.

Because I was well on my way into a broken marriage for some time, God knew my heart and how I felt about forgiveness. He knew of all the anger, resentment, and frustration I had built up inside. But even more so, the incredible thing is that He also knew these feelings were not being completely derived strictly from my disappointments in my marriage and my husband. God knew of all the sorrow and pain I was still carrying from those who had left dark footprints on my heart. God knew something I didn't—He knew that my heart had not yet purely given and forgiven.

So it was through the process of deciphering the words the thoughts and the feelings that this great revelation came to me in the form of understanding two things very clearly. First, that true forgiveness is something we should not continue to carry in our hearts because that simply risks turning it into resentment and anger. Second, understanding how to *let go* of forgiveness is the true meaning of *giving* in its purest form.

Now I encourage you to get comfortable and journey with me because I have something very special I want to share with you. Because like me, your *true* life's journey may very well be getting started the way mine did through the spoken word of a miracle!

The Initial Miracle Request

The words that came from our pastor during our counseling session were simple, straightforward and cut me to the chase. He looked at both my husband and I and said with an almost sorrowful look in his eyes, "You guys need a miracle." So it was right there and right then that I knew, I really knew, that I was *still* on the road to a separation in my marriage, which was ending a fifteen-year-long journey. This separation would start the pulling of levers in all directions for our family as a whole—the type of levers that once pulled can never be pushed back shut because the accumulation of what is about to be poured out outweighed much more of what was left in my marriage.

So there we stood in a small circle in prayer as we always did to close that day's session. I remembered with fear and wept uncontrollably at facing the thoughts of mending not only my broken heart but all of the other pieces of my life. I thought about my future life and how tired I already was, in fact exhausted beyond belief, and wondered how just how was I going to get through this.

Now I believe that it was our pastor's spoken words of needing a miracle, that he was claiming it for us and not just speaking it to us. In the wonders of this world, there are many things that can change our lives and take our breath away and leave us with a sense of awe and wonder. But I also believe that nothing is more powerful than someone speaking spiritual healing and miraculous changes being bestowed into someone's life. It is that level of belief, that confidence and power that can bring the winds of change into someone's life.

You see, what I believed was that I was on the road to destruction, but what someone else believed was that I was on the road to reconstruction. It's really a matter of perspective and the individual's point of view and from God's point of view, a miracle was spoken into our lives by someone who believed in us as a couple and as a family. And when someone believes in you and you believe in your dreams, miracles can happen.

It was February 2008, and as I sat praying over my Bible, pleading with God for a miracle, he brought me to read the following scripture in the book of Joshua, chapter 5:11-12, which reads,

> The day after the Passover, that very day, they ate some of the products of the land: unleavened bread and roasted grain. The manna stopped the day after they ate this food from the land: there was no longer any manna for the Israelites, but that year they ate the produce of Canaan.

The next thing I usually do after reading scripture is thank God for His word and His message to me for that moment on that very day. Then I take those words and meditate on them during the day so I can be reminded in the future of this particular message that God has given me. My expectation is to somehow, and possibly somewhere in time, have those words spoken back into someone else's life who may have a need to hear them at that point of their personal journey.

Now my Bible is one that has a contemporary version, and to fully appreciate and understand the answer God was giving me to my miracle request, I proceeded to read that version very carefully, only to be left feeling sheepish and, needless to say, a bit embarrassed in His eyes for making the overall request. So after reading those words, I took my usual morning bike ride that day feeling a bit disappointed because things just weren't going to happen the way I thought they should. Things weren't going to happen the way I wanted them to happen. Things were simply not going to happen when I expected them to. This miracle wasn't about to be dropped on my lap from God even though He very well could have made it happen that way, but rather, it was going to be given to me in time-in His time.

Because of it, I am here to say that having made the request at that time in my life was truly what started to unfold through more trials and tribulations (and this time they had particular meaning), the biggest life lesson of my personal journey towards His perfect will. This also gave me something deeper in the overall meaning of what I was doing—in asking God for something—and Him giving me in return what I believe a *right heart* truly seeks when asking for the will of God to be fulfilled in one's life, and that is simply a more complete and better understanding of what we ask of Him.

But in that moment on that day, I remember telling some of my friends afterward how I'd actually felt, and it was as if He'd lovingly given me an oh-so-slight tap up the side of the head. You may be wondering why I'd feel that way; after all God loves us and wants to teach us and wants us to learn and grow, which is exactly what started to happen on that day. God wanted me to *understand* the miracle, not simply ask in prayer and faith for something that was within reach (for the miracle is already within me!). He also showed me that prayer is *not* an alternative for preparation and faith is *not* an alternative for hard work. Finally, if my prayers had gone unanswered, perhaps what I needed (my miracle) was within my reach, and I should pray instead for wisdom to see it and the energy and motivation to do it!

Therefore, it is in retrospect and with certain confidence that I say to you that when you call on God to move into your life, do so with an open mind and an open heart—you simply have to be ready to change both! And when your awareness is of having these two entities lined up and working as one in preparation for the receipt of the many blessings that are to come, you will forgo having these many changes from being accompanied by strife.

Now what was about to take place reminds me of the old adage that sometimes in life, things will fall apart in order that they may fall back together again, but this time, it was going to be according to God's plan, to God's will, and most importantly, in God's perfect timing.

Fulfillment of the Request

On February 13, 2009, I wrote, "So there I was stomping my way up the stairs that previous night, telling my husband in a very upset tone of voice, 'I'm going upstairs to read *this* book!" yup, it was all about me trying to somehow maybe prove that this book and these words could have nothing to do with changing my mind about how I felt. I was angry, frustrated, and quite simply fed up and done with my marriage. There was no way I could possibly see myself turning back now. After all, I think I picked up the book and figured I'd check it out simply because our pastor had given it to us that day in our counseling session. Even at that, I had left feeling so upset and so full of tears I didn't even pick it up when we left our session, but my husband did!

Flipping through the first few pages of the book's acknowledgments and other printed material I felt were irrelevant, I made my way to the page I thought I should probably at least read—the introduction. After all, if this author had any type of message that was relevant to my personal situation, I decided that it should at least be capturing my attention right away. Well, it didn't—it seized it! I knew it in my spirit at that very moment that there was something very important for me in these printed words.

I almost felt like I was going to be reading about something very secretive, something that I shouldn't be reading because Satan was going to be very upset if I did! In fact, I felt that way because the first sentence of the introduction read like this. "I can say with absolute confidence that Satan does not want you to read this book" and it was at that very moment that I actually felt a physical change in my body, the type that moves you when you know you've been touched by the Holy Spirit when it is guiding you to do something important. I honestly felt that I was unlocking the door to some secret passage that could possibly lead me to restoration, and God knew how very much I needed that, not only in my marriage, but also in my personal being where it counts the most—in the depths of my very soul.

But like the busy roles that my demanding life always heralds me to be, my son's beck and call swiftly took me away from this immersion I felt I was about to drift into. He'd called me to help him prepare his dinner and, of course, fulfilling yet once again that oh-so-ever-demanding role as a mom, I simply flipped the book shut with a flick on my hand, thinking how it probably wasn't meant to be for me to read more. After all, how much time do we moms, wives, caretakers, cooks, cleaners, laundry washers, bookkeepers—and whatever else you want to fill in here—have to do things such as reading a book? It's like what our pastor said when he gave it to us, "I guess that's all you really need is another book?"

Because I always try to have some form of devotion on a daily basis, that next morning I promised myself that I would simply grab my coffee and reopen the book before checking my e-mails, unloading the dishwasher, or looking at that day's to-do list. So I did. In fact, I sat outside on the porch where I was welcomed by a beautiful day that allowed me to bask in the beauty, warmth, and serenity of the view that lay before me. The lake was peaceful, and the view across the lake, as always, was one that always made me dream. It is the view I envision in my mind's eye when I think of what my Heavenly Father is preparing for me. It is the view of a mansion surrounded by a lush fruit plantation, and because of its physical location, I am blessed with a sunset every night.

So as I comforted myself with the fact that I was allowing myself to escape into this *secret place* with these *secret passages* in words on paper. I had a sense of expectancy that only the blessings of the Lord could bestow upon us when He is about to reveal and move into our lives.

As I read the words, God told me that I was ready not only to be used but to be properly taught about giving. As He once again confirmed in my spirit that He would always make my way audibly clear, I simply asked Him, "Am I ready?" He responded, "You tell me, Are you ready?" I remember feeling a slight angst in my heart, thinking, *Oh no! If I don't answer yes, that may mean more trials and tribulations.* So right there at that very moment I trusted God for His perfect timing in bringing me to the next spiritual realm of my journey. Right then, because of my decision to trust Him, He changed my heart instantly, bringing with it a sense of renewed strength to face whatever it was I had to, once again to fulfill His will for me!

And so it was, but this time He did it through the process of healing. He brought a peace into my heart that led me to have a very civilized, nonconfrontational conversation with my husband that morning. It was truly a gift from God. That was a moment in time when I felt surrounded and truly covered by the blood of Jesus as I poured my heart out in one of the most secure and genuine heartfelt ways that I could ever express myself.

But because I hadn't quite come in grips with the fact that I still had issues from the past regarding the things that plagued my heart, this anger and frustration, which I now had come to realize was my non ability to truly fully forgive, was because of all of the hurt that I'd felt throughout my marriage. My feelings of disbelief at some of the things that my husband had done, some of the decisions he'd made regarding our family, had left me unable to truly find the right outlet to possibly carry on even though I thought I had. But truth be known, I had to find myself completely vulnerable and completely broken to be able to say to my husband that it was I who needed some time to heal.

So the process began with my seeing my husband and two boys off for a road trip to visit my parents-in-law. This was a bit of a sad decision because that weekend, on the Saturday in fact, was Valentine's Day. But the way I saw it and the way that God made me feel about it was that this was going to be time for us. Time for Him to love on me and me to love Him so that He could be there to care for me emotionally as I yet again shed another layer of my former self. I had a sense that the purging of emotions that I had buried so, so far away and deep inside my soul were about to be lifted from me as easily as the gentle flutter of a butterfly's wing, and by grace of God, they were!

And now that the day was over and I sensed how I was feeling at that very moment, I knew that it had been like a flawless play being set up by a master director. My God was anxiously waiting for me to welcome that perfectly orchestrated moment that He had planned for me. As I sat with my eyes gazed onto the pages, it was not what I read that made me ponder, but it was more of the feelings, the deep feelings that accompanied how those words resonated within my soul.

Instantly He touched me. Instantly He began the healing process. Instantly He began another journey for me. Instantly, I began to trust Him in my spirit like I had never trusted Him before!

My Story BIBLE

Before
I
Blew it all and
*L*ost
*E*verything

I suppose you could say that I was truly pointing the finger at my husband for having brought us to the predicament we were in. I felt if only he'd been more of a leader for our family, if only he'd headed up the finances with a better sense of long-term caring, if only he'd been more responsible with the money, if only he'd not wanted to so desperately seek financial independence his way—and now that I know it—instead of the Lord's way. If only, things could have been different today.

I know what the Lord showed me that day was a different perspective from what I'd been used to seeing, living, and feeling. I couldn't so many times and for so many years help but feel a sense of threat, lack of control and disregard from him for his family.

But then God made me realize it's all a matter of perspective, and perspective comes from living in the moment. Some things require projected thought, while other things simply have to be dealt with as best as they can be dealt with at that very moment. Meaning that although I had felt disillusioned, disrespected, and at times taken for granted, my husband's expectations were more often than not those of a man whose heart and mind were for what he thought and felt were for the betterment of his family.

Nonetheless, because I was living in the moment, I had expressed to my husband in our counseling sessions that week much anger and frustration and hurt and deep pain at what had accumulated into our marriage and into our family life. But God reminded me again in a very audible voice that it was not my husband whom I need to trust for the changes in him but that the changes I sought in my husband would be done through Him (the Almighty).

So it was with great hope and great belief and great trust that I asked to be filled with the lessons and the messages that I knew I was ready to learn.

I honestly felt that my spiritual life was about to be catapulted to a place of great wealth and knowledge. I only had to listen. I also knew that because I had surrendered to His perfect will for me, I was being prepared to have my true heart's desire fulfilled. And that is being done right now as you read these words. It had been His perfect timing and His true will to have me venture through the forest for the length of time that I did in order that I may emerge better, brighter, clearer in spirit and ready to spread His light into this world. I can also tell you right now that I felt these are the words that are finally going to print. This was the gift that was given to me in the form of newness to my life. The gift of true courage to write these words and share and tell about my journey so that it may help many more like me who had shunned the idea that it's never too late to start over because *God has your miracle*—and it's only a seed away.

It was with that knowledge that I felt my fingers flying on the keyboard as I let my heart speak without fear. Because it is that fear—the fear that Satan had laced in my heart—that I believed the timing for my purpose had not yet been completed. But I am here to tell you that now is the time for you and if somewhere in your own heart you have been struggling with that, it is through love and support that I do tell you that no other time is better to start listening to God than now! Wherever you are in your spiritual walk with God, know that He is always waiting to guide you, He is always waiting to help you grow, and He is always able to use a willing vessel.

At this time, I am reminded of the following words that I read a while ago, which stirred up the courage in me to star facing the possibility that I in fact did have an important purpose for my life, and these I share with you now:

Our deepest fear is not that we are inadequate. Our deepest fear is that we are powerful beyond measure. It is our light, not our darkness that most frightens us. We ask ourselves, who am I to be brilliant, gorgeous, talented, fabulous? Actually, who are you not to be? You are a child of God. My playing small does not serve the world. There is nothing enlightened about shrinking so that other people won't feel insecure around you. We are all meant to shine, as children do. We were born to make manifest the glory of God that is within us. It's not just in some of us; it's in everyone. And as we let our light shine, we unconsciously give other people permission to do the same. As we are liberated from our own fear, our presence automatically liberates others. (a Return to Love, Marianne Williamson)

The Seeds of Life

Understand that when we plant any kind of seed, it is to be done with the intention of expecting the results we are seeking. We must take that seed and believe in it. We must go about it in a caring fashion, not in a "as the matter of a fact" fashion. With every action, we have an intention, and once we learn to become conscious of our continuous planting and sowing into this world on a daily basis (knowing we are sowing something), the impact into our lives will go beyond what we could have ever imagined.

It is a magnitude beyond what I feel we can truly comprehend. The type of understanding that only our mighty God, who is the Creator of heaven and earth, has the gift of knowing. I believe that if we were able to fully grasp all that we could do while journeying at this time, in this place, we would lose all of our vanities, hatred would be nonexistent, and the word every day of the week would be *love*. Because that in fact is what the Word of God is all about —amore, love!

So I encourage you to think before you speak, think before you do, but most important for now, be kinder to yourself (the personal seed). Life can throw many things our way that sometimes leave us feeling like we've been in a war ourselves, and the scars that are behind can be very deep—in fact, so deep that only the supernatural power of

God's healing hand and His love are the cures for our ailing hearts.

When you think of it, it's usually rather small. It makes its way from soil to sky in a time period that will eventually, if planted in good soil, come to fruition. I believe that our lives and all of the events in it are very much like seeds. They allow us to grow through the process of these circumstances, and if we are well connected spiritually, they usually bring some form of exponential growth personally that become our seeds for the future in God's kingdom.

The greatest part of that is when we realize the number of people we can impact with just one seed. When planted with love, caring, and precision, that effort can and will bring results that we wouldn't even dare to imagine because at times, unfortunately, we think that we aren't even worthy of that! But I'm here to tell you that because our lives are very much like a seed, and God made us that seed, it is completely up to us to decide how and when to feed it, water it, and care for it. We are His creation, and because He did plant us at the time that He did, we should be forever grateful. It is part of His will, and His timing for us. *What* we do with that seed within us, and *how much* we do with it, is completely up to us. We have the capability of touching very many or very few lives.

I strongly urge you to look closely at the life of Jesus Christ. He was the son of a carpenter. He only started to minister at the age of thirty up to a period of three years when He died at the age of thirty-three. He never held an office, and He never traveled more than two hundred miles away from his home town of Bethlehem, no other leader, king, or politician in the history of this world has impacted the universe more than this single solitary life! To this day, He is known so much in this world, and his seed is still impacting the lives of many and more to come.

I believe we all have that same potential, and if we could understand the true importance of living our lives to the fullest, we would be doing the same. I also believe that the *light* seed, the one we may think is irrelevant or unimportant, is one of the most important seeds of life. This seed can bring change into someone's life and possibly help create a huge ripple effect in the world, just like Jesus did. When you look at what He took time to do most, you realize that you don't have to be rich or a scholar or strong or head of a Fortune 500 company or a celebrity or from the right side of the tracks or have a particular color of skin or live in a particular neighborhood. You just have to take the time to *do* it! To listen, to love, to care!

It's having a daily routine of consciously spending your light through the sowing of smile, a gentle touch, a kind word, or a thoughtful gesture. You just never know who you will meet on a particular day whose life you may change or impact because you took the time to say hello or were kind enough to hold a door open for them. You just never know how deep your thoughtful way will impact someone's day by asking from the heart, "So how are you feeling today?"

The Spirit Walker

And that is exactly how our pastor had always started our counseling sessions—by asking us, "So how are you guys doing today?" When you think of it, you might be saying to yourself that this would be a pretty standard type of question, considering we were in counseling. After all, we were there to talk about matters of the heart and our usual answers ranged from "All right" to "Well, we're here!" But today was different. Today I had a story to tell. Something incredible had happened to me over the weekend, and I was sitting at the edge of my chair on pins and needles just waiting to share it with our counseling pastor.

So there I sat in all *my* glory, beaming from ear to ear, just waiting with full anticipation for the moment when I was able to speak. Well, that wasn't too long because I love to talk, express myself, and always be bearer of good news when possible! So I did, and my eyes grew big, my lips pulled outward into a great big smile, and as I could feel my heart soaring, I spoke the words that he had spoken to us.

"Pastor Gary," I said, like a small child anticipating a love tap on my head simply for speaking up, "I received a miracle from God this weekend!"

Then he was the one who smiled back, and his eyes grew bigger, and I believe that it was in *that* very moment that his heart was soaring as well at the thought of us being there with good news. I then proceeded to tell him what happened—how I almost didn't read the book but eventually did, only because I felt it was out of obligation. But now that God had changed my heart and given me revelation into my marriage from just the first twenty-two pages of this book, I was thrilled and ecstatic to tell him how grateful I was that he had in fact gifted us with the book.

Well, to our surprise, he's the one who proceeded to tell us how he had actually hesitated in giving us the book. He explained it was because we were discussing issues of bankruptcy (losing) and this book talked about giving. Then he said God put it on his heart this time to give it to us anyway. He presented it to us saying, "Here's a book I'd like to give you. I guess that's all you really need is another book? But I know you both are givers and it talks about having a blessed life and I know you both deserve to have a blessed life."

Needless to say, that sparked up a whole new other conversation in which he also shared the fact that the copy he gave us (which was technically his second copy because his first was being shipped in the mail) was the one he'd obtained at a pastor's meeting that very same morning! Now in retrospect, imagine how I felt at the idea that he'd almost not "asked" for a copy of the book. Would I be sitting here typing these words? I don't know! Would I be excited at this time simply knowing that I now have an opportunity to spread my light in the world for God's kingdom through the future publication of this book? I highly doubt it!

You see, what I'm trying to enlighten you with is this: when your intentions are good and your heart is pure, good things can come from all that you do. But it's when you don't realize or simply are not fully aware that what you are about to do is change someone's life direction, then, just then, know that you have been touched to receive one of the biggest blessings you could ever be honored with—that of the Spirit Walker.

Life's trials and tribulations are not for us to personally carry as if they were our very own, because they are not! Jesus was given to us for that very cause. He was nailed to a cross, and His blood was extracted from His body, torn from His flesh through suffering and pain, so that when we live in this world, we do not have to suffer as He did. He was made to bring us through them, and it is our responsibility to bring them to His feet *daily*. It pains me now and quickens my heart when I realize that we do not take full advantage of the victory that was given to us. The *power* that the blood of Jesus is undeniably life changing!

I remember viewing a television channel roughly two years ago that showed a picture of a young Bill Graham sitting by a riverbed on some rock with two men from a local village some place in Africa. What I distinctly remember from that episode, in conjunction with having that picture still etched in my mind, was the question the interviewer asked Mr. Graham. He said, "Mr. Graham, if you were to start all over again, is there anything you would change, anything you would do different?" at which Mr. Graham replied, "I would talk more about the cross. I would talk more about the cross and the blood of Jesus."

To this day, I have carried that moment in my heart and carried it like a torch—for Jesus! I know I could never even fathom to even consider sacrificing either one of my two boys through any type of pain and physical torture and suffering to save the world in helping grow God's kingdom. Even though I know the outcome of having *that* seed planted by God for all of mankind and especially as a mother, I know that my sinful and selfish nature would have immediately surfaced, and it's because of that knowledge that I return to God the best way that I possibly can, in the only way that I can, the expression of my love—through the way of the Spirit Walker.

God's daily mercy and grace is what can and will keep you moving forward!

Forces of darkness will and are always on the lookout for those of us who are growing His Kingdom.

*Put on your Armor!
Pick up your shield and sword!
Stand tall, be strong and courageous!*

There is much work to be done and time is not on our side.

-C. W.

PART II

THE SECOND BOOK OF LIFE:

THE SPIRIT WALKER
HOW TO BECOME A WARRIOR FOR GOD'S KINGDOM

Introduction

Helping You toward Your Destiny through
Faith and a Commitment for Greater Purpose

I closed my eyes and took a slow sip from my first cup of coffee, and it felt so good to just unwind, relax, and start to decompress. I had finally made it! I had gotten in late the night before, and even though I was feeling a bit mentally and emotionally battered and bruised, I knew with every fiber of my being that this time was truly going to happen. How could it not? I had the environment and the time, but most importantly, I had the love and support of my new family.

Books, a lot of books, are written to tell or share a story that have positive results. This book is not any different, and although it may not seem like it to some, the ones who walk the narrow path will be able to identify with and connect to what is about to be revealed to them. Those of you who have never been given the opportunity to learn about this path are being offered it right now.

The Sower's Harvest

It has been a long time, and so much has been kept inside that I am now ready to release all that has been captured. Many thoughts and feelings through much time can create a story that each one of us can tell. Mine is probably not much more different than many of your life journeys. A common thread that so many of us share is our basic need to be made to feel acknowledged in life. Whether as a parent, a teacher, a prince, or a pauper, there is nothing more empowering than being made to feel like we belong.

For all of those moments when you've simply asked yourself why, the writing of the Second Book of Life is especially for you. After all, timing is everything, and with a combination of conscious sowing and an open mind, I believe that the time has come for you to belong too. Most importantly, it is simply for you to know that in the end, you too can live happily ever after whatever may come your way!

Prelude to Steps of the Spirit Walker

Let me begin by sharing the fact that since the "First book of Life," things have change for me, and I am here now to let you know that I stand in victory. Although what has unveiled in the last several years had initially left my vision short of that, I can tell you with absolute certainty that the path of my life has been consistently guided through God's revelations to me.

You see, the most important thing I have come to realize and want to share with you, first and foremost, is that no one's life is perfect, and because of that, God loves you exactly where you are! The whole mess of you—your mistakes, your bad choices, your continued sin—He will forgive you of all these every time you ask when you seek Him every day of your life!

It is truly a blend. I know because I had been in bondage to a state of mind for years, thinking that if only a certain thing could be a certain way, before I felt like I could contribute the way I could, should, and overall, simply wanted to! You see, when you're a giver, there is nothing worse than feeling like you have nothing to "give" of yourself! Satan led me to believe that. The simple fact that this book had not materialized before now is proof of that, but the greatest thing of all to come out of that situation is the fact that what Satan intended for evil, God used for His will in my life. Please remember that because it is a powerful thought process that not only changes your mind but empowers your way of living. So remember to not only ask why, but ask, "Why not?" and trust God to let Him use you through that season of your life so that you can bless others in the future! When you get, give. When you learn, teach. Pass it on!

So to all of you who feel that your sense of true purpose is not being fulfilled or that you are not even near what you think you should be doing, think again! The Lord God is always keeping you on track. Whether we think we are or we think we are not, we are both. Whatever path we choose for ourselves, it is always in sync with God's plans. Whatever stray path we are on, God will be there too. There will never be a time that God does not use whatever we are going through to fulfill His needs for us. It is truly hard to imagine at times that wherever we are is part of what we're predestined for, but that is the true love of God showing us that when we stick to Him like glue, the bond cannot be broken and our path cannot misguided.

In the end she knew she had walked the chosen path. It had come with a heavy price to pay, but the reward that awaited her at the end of this long journey was more than worth it.

This time it was another path, which was filled with certainty, accompanied by clarity, and most important it was represented by inner peace.

The type she felt when she had been in the presence of God Himself!

That of...
The Spirit Walker

Spoken Silence

You see, things had actually gotten even worse for us before they got better. In fact I remember when we had an estate sale, we met some buyers who said they had gone through very similar circumstances and expressed words of encouragement to us through our times of trials and tribulations. It brought temporary solace, and I received the empathy with sincerity, but I knew what and whom I would have to reach out to in order to survive this—God's word and presence!

Because there are certain things you just never want to go through in your lifetime, let alone write about them in an open book, I choose to do so because I want you to understand the depth of the pit I was in and how God's mercy and grace lifted me out of there.

First, you'll never want to have to sell your favorite jewelry to pay your power bill. Second, you'll never want to have to sell your furniture to celebrate Christmas. Finally—the worst thing you'll ever have to need to do—is raid your kid's bank accounts to put food on the table. These are some of the things that when I stop and think about them, I realize how harmful, painful, and devastating they were to go through. This I would never wish on anymore, but this is exactly what I had to do to survive! So one day I decided I had enough of doing this on my own, so I took a knee and prayed and asked God with a wrench-filled heart to take over my life, and He did!

After the loss of both our businesses and income in 2008, things, shall we say, started to unravel rather quickly. Once again, levers had been pulled, and nothing could stop the speed at which our lives were being torn apart.

First, our homes were repossessed and finally released through short sales, the plight of many at this time in life after the real estate crash of 2008. Second, we had to file for bankruptcy, which really puts you in a dark place, stagnant almost, because you are forced to become still for a period of time while "legal matters ensue." It is also the time when your self-esteem gets attacked the most, layer by layer, until you feel at times worthless.

Then because employment was difficult to find and in order for us to even survive, we had to ask my then husband's parents if we could move back in with them. If there was ever a time for reality to kick in and have you truly feel the descent you are about to fall into, this was it. Please know that we were very grateful for the blessing of family at that time in our lives; it's just that this setback has way of bringing you to your knees, which I can honestly tell you now is not such a bad place to be, and God knew that!

But what I didn't know—and He was about to reveal to me—was the succession of "words of knowledge" that He wanted me to bring forth through the writing of this book. So as I prepared myself to be submerged into a depth of spirituality that I had yet to experience, I brought along with me my bare soul, my quiet spirit, and my hungry heart, all of which He would feed the Revelation of the Scrolls.

After all, I needed to be well prepared for what still lay ahead—the loss of our family cars, one by one; me leaving my family in one city so I could pursue work and employment in another, which by the way, as a mom leaving your children behind, is not an easy thing to do. I still remember, and it still saddens me when I think of how I felt, when my brain quite literally could not compute not having my children in my daily life. I remember struggling with the simple fact that I could not grasp or understand why the emotional and mental state I was in was because of the distance between me and my sons. I can honestly say it was one of the most difficult and heart-wrenching thing I could ever go through, have ever gone through, and would never want to experience again!

Shortly afterwards was the rental of a home with no furnishings, except for a couch loaned to us by our landlord and a television set that sat on the floor—that was our living room setup! Our kid's beds had been given to us (thanks JZ), and I had bent over every night in tears to try and get comfortable to sleep on our air mattress, which would deflate and have me waking up on the floor every morning.

Donations of food and clothing were also a regiment to our lifestyle during these years, and I can honestly say that I was continually grateful but was always waiting for the floodgates of heaven to open up so I could once again be on the flip side of this picture. After all, losing a six-figure income and going from riches to rags will hopefully leave you feeling passionate about regaining that ground. Financial independence, depending on how you handle it, can be a blessed life for you and others! I never stopped believing, I kept on praying, and my faith never wavered; it may have weakened, but I never wavered from the rock that I stood on—never!

In the end—and there was an ending before the new beginning—the craziest situation was when I had to move back in with my ex-husband because of my loss of employment and roommate and I could no longer afford to live where I was. Therefore, it was once again with a grateful heart for the help I received that we—my now ex-husband and two teenage boys and a dog—lived together in his fifteen-feet-wide-by-thirty-feet-long trailer. This was now home. Every night, we had to blow up my oldest son's single air mattress bed, and every morning, we had to store it! I slept next to him on a small couch that was shorter than me and had to prop my legs up and put my feet on the wall if I wanted to sleep on my back!

We did this for almost four months, but always looking ahead, I knew this was all temporary. Therefore, my joy could not be taken because I knew what still lay ahead, and because of that, my peace never left me. I was always looking to see how God would work my way out of this, and He did!

PART III

REVELATION OF THE SCROLLS

SCROLL 1:
The Approach (Attitude)

Above all else, guard your heart, for it is the wellspring of life.
Proverbs 4:23

A
T*ime*
To
I*ntroduce*
T*rue*
U*nderlying*
D*esires*
E*xponentially*

Attitude is a choice and when you make it a good one stand back, watch and see what happens.

–C. W.

From Surrendering to Stripped Away

It is with extreme certainty now that I have come to learn and grow from surrendering it all to God. It is with the right attitude, a grateful and humble heart, that I know how much He truly loves me, by how much He strips away from me. I say this because I know now that when we completely surrender to God and honestly want to have Him bring changes into our lives, He will do so and often at a price that we are not quite willing or *expecting* to pay. But when God needs us to change, it does not mean it is from the head, but it rather is from the heart, where change is needed most.

I personally do not believe that He wants us to surrender unless we are completely willing to trust Him. It is from this trust, along with the right attitude, that we gather our strength, and it is from this strength that we grow closer to Him, and that is exactly where He wants us to be—closer to Him, especially in our greatest times of need.

It can truly hard, I know, to fully understand this cycle, but it is one that I have experienced many times now. My repeated efforts in "letting go and surrendering it all in times of great need" have brought me a depth of peace that only our God could bestow upon us. It is His gift to us;

otherwise, as His children, we could not bring ourselves, as many children do, to trust Him the way He wants us to, and I must underline that we must trust Him for absolutely everything!

It is not sufficient enough to know that He will provide for our tomorrow, but it is sufficient to know that He will provide for us today because that is where He lives—is here with us now, right now, for today. I think once we realize that He is the great I Am, that He does not live in our failed past, nor does He live in our worrisome tomorrow, only then will we feel the peace that He so desperately wants us to dwell in.

There is nothing more powerful like being in the present. Stop right now and look around you and be grateful for what you've got; don't focus on what you don't have. Take what you've already got and see how much you can do with it; don't look at what you don't have and think you don't have enough to do something to still make an impact because this is where God is right now!

I Am

*I was regretting the past
and fearing the future.
Suddenly my Lord was speaking:
"My name is I AM." He paused.
I waited. He continued,
"When you live in the past
with its mistakes and regrets,
it is hard. I am not there.
My name is not I WAS.
When you live in the future,
with its problem and fears,
it is hard. I am not there.
My name is not I WILL BE.
When you live in this moment,
it is not hard. I am here.
"My name is I AM."*

Helen Mallicoat

SCROLL 2:
THE SACRED TIME
(TRUST)

Be Still and Know that I Am God.
Psalm 46:10

Take

Rest

Unto

Sanctified

Time

The amount of rest you have in your spirit is a direct reflection of the amount of trust you put in God.
—C. W.

It came as no surprise to her that her fingers were furiously typing across the keyboard. With her eyes shut, inspirational music in the background, she felt the anointing and simply sat down and wrote. A message from God himself, she knew she had to do it at the time He gave her these revelations because it was then that the Spirit Walker dwelled the strongest. It comforted her, it gave her a connection, it brought peace during these very sacred times that she cherished so dearly.

She knew that God had given her a specific job to do, and with time, experience, trials and tribulations, and a never-ending hunger to gain wisdom from the Word of God, she came out of it more alive then she could have ever imagined.

She was *victorious*. She was a *winner*. She had been shown through the process of *being still* and having the *right attitude*, what it was that she could bring to her heavenly father's kingdom. The most important thing she learned was the key is knowing the attitude that you keep while being still, which makes all the difference in the world.

To trust God means to trust Him even when we don't understand why events occur as they do, nor the need to understand it all.

You must rest during the time that God is keeping you waiting because it is that rest that will bring you peace, and then it is that peace that then shows God that you are in fact trusting Him completely.

You must be solid during this time also because it is during this season which is as important as what the season brings itself, that you must trust the *time* He is taking to make things happen. Habakkuk 2:3 reads, "For the revelation awaits an appointed time; it speaks of the end and will not prove false."

It Isn't Easy to be Patient

When God showed me this scripture, He revealed himself to me! Not only that He was in control of my life (still), but much more importantly, He showed me His heart. He showed me how much harder it is for Himself to be patient because, you see, He knows the plans He has for us! Not only does He know, He knows exactly *when* His plans will come to pass for us. So when you think you're about to give up on yourself, your life, your dreams, and your goals, remember this: it is much harder for God to be patient than it is us. Now just stop for a moment, be *present*, and really think about that!

How much harder can it be for a loving, caring, and giving Father, who knows all the answers we are seeking to find, to see us suffering so much, hurting so much, questioning so much, falling to pieces, losing faith, and losing hope! He prays that we do not give up; He prays that we hang in there until His timing comes to pass. He aches in His heart at the prospect of losing us to defeat, of losing us to alcoholism, of losing us to drugs or prostitution, of losing us to gambling it all away, or for falling into someone else's arms! He cries and hurts inside too when He sees that we are about to give up on our promises, our hope, and our dreams! He cries as any parent would at the thought of losing a child!

The Sower's Harvest

So it is with certainty that I write these words to you now to tell you that

When you feel that time of despair
remember to simply look up in the air,
for it is there that I will be looking down at you,
seeking you out, to confirm, explain and tell you
what to do!

Never give up on me when you are seeking answers,
just remember to dwell in the place where you really
matter,
in my presence there is hope, love and reassurance
and it is also where you get your crown of
endurance.

For during the time of trials and tribulations,
is when I seek you out most for this duration.
So know that *I AM* with you in spirit and soul,
and I will continue to do so until you grow old!

And whenever that time will happen to be,
remember to always "hang on to me."
For you are my children, my daughter, my son,
and from my perspective, the only one!
So never lose patience and remember this always,
I will continue to care,
until the day I carry you up in the air.

Your Loving Father

SCROLL 3: THE INHERITANCE (MIRACLES)

If you believe, you will receive whatever you ask for in prayer.
Matthew 21:22

My

Inheritance

Reproduces

Abundance

Continuously

Lovingly, and is

Everlasting!

Never underestimate the size of the miracle God delivers to you.

–C. W.

The power of prayer can move mountains. They are the beginning of your miracles.

They are the *superhighways* to heaven. Let God open the floodgates of heaven for you so you can claim your inheritance early—because you can!

The kind of prayer that moves mountains is prayer for the fruitfulness of God's kingdom. God will answer your prayers, but not as a result of your positive mental attitude. Other conditions must be met.

- You must be a believer.
- You must not hold a grudge against another person.
- You must not pray with selfish motives.
- Your request must be for the good of God's kingdom.

To pray effectively, you need faith in God, not faith in the object of your request. If you focus on your request, you will be left with nothing if your request is refused.

On Powerful Prayer: The Miracle Inheritance

Please excuse yourself!

You know, most of the time, what God has in store for us is right in front of us. All we have to do is get out of our own way! To fully realize and comprehend that God is a loving and giving God is undeniable. I mean, when was the last time that you saw Him do something you asked? How awesome was that?

What about its timing? Did you ever deny the belief that your prayers had been answered because whatever you prayed for happened instantaneously? Let me assure you that once you ask, God moves! What we have to do about receiving our answers through prayer is kick up our level of belief. When we continue to ask for the same thing over and over again, it's because we never believed that God moved in the first place! The fact is that God releases and answers prayer in Jesus's name.

God's timing is always a factor in this equation because when God releases, the timing as to when our physical world receives it is always perfect. Be it instantaneous or not, God's timing is always perfect, and I cannot stress this enough, and you have to believe that too. If we don't receive our answers, it's probably because there is something "interrupting" its delivery—very likely ourselves.

What I have come to understand is that Satan will take every opportunity to intercede and mess up the delivery. What we have to do about it is *not* continuously ask for the same thing over and over again, but rather pray for its delivery. Believing that it's on its way (always in God's perfect timing). We are often so caught up in being doubtful and unbelievers in God's power that we ourselves are the culprits in not having what truly belongs to us! No job, no home—no circumstance cannot be changed or attained if we simply, pray, ask, believe, and then get out of our own way! And this begins with the right attitude. You see, what begins in your mind affects what happens in your heart, and then its effects are felt by what we speak!

So when we pray, we have to be able to wrap our heads around the fact that where we allow our minds to go in prayer—the level at which we can honestly believe in God's power—will affect our emotions during prayer, and that is where you "belief" comes from. But it's not from the head because that's your starting point. It's from the heart, where God dwells in you most. If God doesn't dwell in your heart (the heart of your spirit) Then He wouldn't given us one. He'd simply, I believe, given us a head to "understand" who He is, but the fact is that He gave us a heart to *know* who He is. He wants us to know Him; He wants us to be overwhelmed physically in that everlasting, glorious feeling of jubilee that can overtake our bodies when we are in the presence of His Holy Spirit!

Another thing God has shown me is that your everyday life is critical in relation to your prayer request. You might ask, how is that relative? Because the anointing of God's blessings on our lives can be interceded by the powers of darkness, we must realize that everyday life is very relative to our prayers. First, there is the fact that you must be a steward of your own words. If you have asked God for something in prayer, in the spirit, and then follow up with nonbelief in your attitude and actions once you are out of that realm in your everyday life, you are quite literally jeopardizing its delivery!

There are so many components in our lives that have made us who we are, and for the most of us, there's a story, there's a mess, there have been issues. By God's grace, our salvation has released us from sin, death and disease. But because our natural and human tendencies lean quicker to worldly ways than spiritual ways, it has become a true barrier for us to believe that what we pray for in the flesh would ever be delivered to us from the spirit realm.

It is important that we accept that we are spirits before we are flesh in order that our connection into God's world be reflected in ours. What I mean is that although we are physical, fleshy beings, we must be able to bring ourselves to that level of knowledge, confidence, and boldness that God requires us to collect for ourselves so that He can move in the ways we want Him to!

Again, being sinners and imperfect and saved has given us that highway to heaven, where we can now look forward to eternal life, but God wants more for us. In fact He wants so much more. He wants us to experience heaven here on earth. He doesn't want us to have to wait to leave the earthy realm in order for us to experience His spiritual blessings. And that is why He gave us prayer, and that is why Jesus taught the disciples how to pray, and within that prayer is a temple for us to use whenever we reach out for bigger things than we could ever attain for ourselves!

Being believable and true to ourselves, we should know all things we do are through Christ. Every moment of every day, we should acknowledge our weakness and fear God for who He is in relation to who we are. Psalm 25:12 reads, "Who then, is the man that fears the Lord? He will instruct him in the way chosen for him."

That is why prayer is such an important tool to a person's arsenal. Not only does God want us to come to Him in prayer, but He also relishes the fact that we are able to ask Him—because we love Him—through prayer for guidance with every detail of our day.

How many times have you earnestly, wholeheartedly, believing 110 percent, asked God to bless you with a perfect parking spot and got it!

How did you feel at that moment? Was it believable to you? Did you know better than to stand in your own way mentally and not believe it could happen, or did you have a bit of positive attitude in knowing that God can make this happen for you?

I use this example lightly, but in reality, it's just us looking at the surface (not even scratching it yet) that gives us a glimpse into what the Lord our God has in store for us here and now!

Prayer is a supernatural highway that He has created not just for us but most importantly for Him. God almighty wants us to come to Him like a child and ask—simply ask with an open mind, a softened heart, and the capability of speaking it into our lives because we are worthy, deserving, and we are the proof that this is how He shows his love for us! Until we are in God's perfect world, living in God's perfect presence, it is His will that we open our hearts and our minds to what He knows we can be blessed with. We simply have to have the right

- attitude (your mind)—it is easier to change your mind, than it is to change how you feel;
- belief (your heart)—when your dreams are bigger than your past, it allows you to live into the future; and
- conviction (your tongue)—remember that words are like fire. You can neither control nor reverse the damage they can do!

So the next time you come to God in prayer to *ask* for something, approach it this way.

Teach me Father as only you can do,
to help me *relearn* my ABCs
so that I can be blessed by you!

SCROLL 4: THE STILLNESS

Delight yourself in the Lord and he will give you the desires of your heart. Commit your way to the Lord; trust in him and he will do this.
Psalm 37:4-5

Chosen
Opportunities
Make
Me
Identify
The
Momentum
Extended to
Navigate my
Tomorrows!

Commitment to something is a decision only you have the power to make.

−C. W.

How do we become successful?
By committing ourselves to what we want to achieve.

How do we commit?
By preparing the soil of our hearts.

How do we prepare our hearts?
By making God number one in our hearts and putting our trust and faith in Him.

Hear Me, See Me, Feel Me

He always has something He wants us to hear, He always has something He is trying to show us, and if we are well connected, He wants us to feel it too!

How *great* is our God! How can we claim to have God on our side when we never take enough time, or any time for that matter, in the busyness of our lives to stop and listen, hear and feel what it is that He is trying to communicate to us?

Now that my faith had expanded exponentially, I was truly grateful that I had chosen to be submerged in a place where I knew He was always bound to show up through His promises to me. I had taken for granted too long the fact that I have a God who is always willing and waiting to show me the way and I, in return, have never stepped up to the place where He waits for me.

I would like to encourage all of us to commit the time that we need to tap into what has been given to us on a silver platter and then some! Why not believe that we are worthy of the best of what He has to give us? Why not claim all of victories that He has already paid the price for?

Personally, I think that in our thoughts of unworthiness, topped off with a sprinkle of the enemy, we relinquish what is ours on a daily basis, and that is a sad shame. So because I had come to a place that had left me with no other choice but to seek Him for everything every day as I got through these tumultuous times, I want to share with you something He showed me one day as we were having a conversation—oh yes, He does talk to us if we stop long enough to listen, did you know that?

First, I declared my commitment to this personal change in my life because of these storms. I committed myself to living no other way but the way of God. As His child, I promised to come to Him exactly the way He wanted me to—humble and with a childlike heart!

You see, I know now beyond (and that's really far away) the shadow of any doubt that this is the way we are to live. Our spirit dwells within us and is very often confused by the flesh that surrounds us, but make no mistake that these are two very separate entities. It is when we fully realize and grasp this truth that I believe we can start to tap into our victories even more intensely!

So for all of those moments when we feel like we are in a blender at high speeds not knowing what we are experiencing and why we are going through certain things, try exercising the attitude of victory that God has already stamped on us. It's okay—we've been approved for it!

Therefore I tell you, do not worry about your life, what you will eat or drink; or about your body, what you will wear. Is not life more important than food, and the body more important than clothes? Look at the birds of the air; they do not sow or reap or store away in barns, and yet your heavenly Father feeds them. Are you not much more valuable than they? Who of you by worrying can add a single hour to his life? And why do you worry about clothes? See how the lilies of the field grow. They do not labor or spin. Yet I tell you that not even Solomon in his entire splendor was dressed like one of these. If that is how God clothes the grass of the field, which is here today and tomorrow is thrown in the fire, will he not much more clothe you, O you of little faith? So do not worry, saying, 'What shall we eat?' or 'What shall we drink?' or 'What shall we wear?' For the pagans run after all these things, and your heavenly Father knows that you need them. But seek first His kingdom and His righteousness, and all these things will be given to you as well.

Matthew 6:25-33

So here is the conversation I had with God on that beautiful, clear, and sunny morning.

As I was walking back toward the house, having taken the dog for a walk by the lake, I told God, "You know, Lord, I feel like I am naked. I feel like I am starting all over again with nothing, like a baby coming out of a womb, needing to count on her mother for everything."

He replied, "And you are going to rely on me for everything, and I am going to take care of you."

I let out a small whimper, and whether it was out of relief or sadness, all I know is that I not only brought it to His feet right there and then once again, but gave myself permission to simply bask in the feeling of comfort that came along with having my Heavenly Father tell me loud and clear that everything was going to be okay and that everything was going to be all right and that everything was going to work out.

If I could put a penny in a jar for every time He tried telling me that...

If I could put a penny in a jar for every time He tried showing me that...

If I could put a penny in a jar for every time He tried to make me feel that...

I'd be a richer person in spirit and now that I know, I have claimed my fortune!
-C. W.

We all learn in different ways, I know, and it is my hope for you today that you become more aware of your surroundings, and if you stop long enough, I know that God will show up sometime, somehow. So stop, look, listen, and feel!

When we just don't give up on something and commit ourselves to it, we are bound to get desired end results. Sometimes that end result is nothing more than another step, another layer that we are to pass through in order to make our way to a new revelation. God never gives up on us, so why do we give up on ourselves so easily? Persistence, accompanied by pushing through pain, will always birth something new!

SCROLL 5: THE EMBRACE (FAITH)

God presented him as a sacrifice of atonement, through faith in his blood. He did this to demonstrate his justice, because in his forbearance he had left the sins committed beforehand unpunished.
Romans 3:26

Forge
Ahead
Insatiably
Toward
Heaven

Faith is not an emotion; it is a powerful spiritual force that impacts God's realm.

-C. W

Because
Everyday
Life
Involves
Embracing
Victories
Every day

Believe in yourself first—it will make way for others to believe in you too!

-C. W

Can You Imagine

Can you imagine the level of faith to live in a time when all you had were prophetic words that encouraged you to believe in your salvation only by *looking forward in faith* to the coming of Christ…

Can you imagine the level of faith to live without even knowing Jesus's name or the details of his earthly life, only by *looking forward in faith* to receiving your salvation…

Reading this scripture had left me feeling so inspired to elevate my personal level of faith!

I cannot imagine the level of faith it must have taken to believe in salvation with only the spoken words of prophets—how hard it must have been! How difficult yet so triumphant the flesh must have been in resisting and crushing one's faith. The devil must have had a heyday purging people's thoughts on faith simply by discharging any idea of a forthcoming savior!

My heart was saddened at that moment but encouraged at the same time. It was saddened because when I think of all of those who had to walk that *walk of faith* for the belief of their salvation without knowing what is known now! And now when I look at how incredibly difficult it is today for people in this world, at this time, to have enough courage to try to walk this same walk of faith, that of the Spirit Walker, for the same salvation, even after prophecies have been fulfilled, even after the blood has been shed, even after the Lord Christ has been risen, I have to ask myself,

Can you imagine the level of faith it must have taken for those who walked before Christ did, for those who believed before Christ came, for those who fought the ultimate fight of the flesh, for those who stood steadfast in their beliefs for salvation (against nonbelievers and Satan) for those who did—what a victory it has been!

So my prayer for the world today is that to all of those who walk the walk of faith, be blessed in knowing that not only do you have salvation in Christ but that you are covered in His blood, which was the ultimate sacrifice for our sins! And also be encouraged in knowing that *looking forward in faith* is not just an attitude but a way for you to bring salvation to others because it is this attitude that will gather the lost souls of this world.

Blessed is he that looks forward in faith!
Blessed is he that walks the walk of faith!
Blessed is he that shares the word of God!

Believe that faith and Christ's resurrection power that lives in you are the greatest power in the world.

Faith [noun]: belief in, devotion to, or trust in somebody or something, especially without logical proof.

Power [noun]: the ability, strength and capacity to do something, influence over other people and their actions.

(*Encarta Dictionary:* English (North America)

To believe in God that has the ability, strength, and capacity to influence our actions without logical proof is powerful faith.

Always look for God inside of your trials and tribulations because it is during these times that He will guide you to those you can minister to—making you selfless in action and growing His kingdom.

SCROLL 6: THE CHANGE OF HEART (LOVE)

Love the Lord your God with all your heart and with all your soul and with all your mind and with all your strength.
Mark 12:30-31

Let

Others

View

Eternity through You!

Love in the morning, love in the evening, love all day long.

—C. W.

Feeling Guilty—Almost but Not Quite!

God is so amazing! I'm always in awe when the things He promises me show up in my life. But then again, why should I be? I know what His words says because "it is written." So then why am I so surprised that He's come to my rescue, that He's answered my prayers? I think it's because every single time He does something amazing, He simply reminds me of how very deep, wide, high, and unending His love truly is for me! And in my books, that's enough to bring me to my knees and cry.

How deep is your love for Him?

What would it take for you to do something so incredible for someone that they would fall down to their knees and verbally express their unending love back to you?

Could we do it?

Are we able to?

Do we have the consciousness to do it?

Do we have the courage to do it?

Are we strong enough to do it?

Do we love God enough to do it?

The Sower's Harvest

My friends, I only hope that we do. Because I believe with all my heart and soul that our daily life on this planet is to take every opportunity we have to touch the suffering people of this world. It is with kindness and compassion for others that we will be given compassion in return. It is with love in our hearts and a song in our souls that our light will shine and as we do, we will permit others to do the same.

He showed me something one day. He showed me something so powerful that I believe it actually changed my personal view of God—not my overall view of Him, simply who He is, what He wants to give us, and how desperately He wants to do it!

As I read a scripture one morning, something happened at one point. I was so hungry for His word that I read more scriptures than I usually did and had an overflow going on in my spirit, and this is what He revealed to me through the Holy Spirit.

Hunger for his word
and He will fill you with his living waters
overflowing from your soul,
bathing you in an emotional lift
that only God could bestow upon you.
Maybe this was just for you.
Maybe this was just for me.
Maybe this was for all of us.

What He also showed me that day was a new perspective on His word. You see, I've always felt this was His way of leaving us His legacy for us to learn from, which is true. But the understanding that really enlightened me was this word from Him.

I did leave you a legacy.
I simply want you to understand…
That when you read My Word,
That is I, witnessing to you.

As I typed these words and grasped their full meaning, he apprehended me once again, and I thanked Him!

I knew in that very moment that I would never be able to capture all of the love and all of the beauty that He has in store for me. I know my heavenly warehouse will have many unopened boxes in it unfortunately, but I do hope that I will have a chance to open them someday. And so I expressed to Him that I didn't care to understand anymore why or how what He does is done—I simply wanted to live it!

SCROLL 7: THE SEED (DOING)

And you were also included in Christ when you heard the word of truth the gospel of your salvation. Having believed, you were marked in him with a seal, the promised Holy Spirit, who is a deposit guaranteeing our inheritance until the redemption of those who are God's possession—to the praise of his glory.
Ephesian 1:13-14

Serve

Everyone

Equally and

Desirably

Remember to always water your seed.

−C. W.

The Guiding Seed

The Holy Spirit is God's seal that we belong to Him and His deposit guaranteeing that He will do what He has promised.

The Holy Spirit is like a down payment, a deposit validating signature on the contract.

The presence of the Holy Spirit in us demonstrates the genuineness of our faith, proves that we are God's children, and secures eternal life for us. His power works in us to transform us now, and what we experience now is a taste of the total change we will experience in eternity.

God's Revelation to Me on Sowing

God made us all farmers of our own land, to sow and create our very own divinely designed world. He also gave us an invisible pair of overalls; we just don't know we are wearing them. So, in fact, we could sow, sow, sow everywhere we go—in the grocery store, at the mall, in the boardroom, and even down the hall.

You have the power to create, and that power was given to each and everyone of us to use with unlimited boundaries. If we stopped long enough to realize that there are endless opportunities for us to sow and collect a harvest from just by looking outside of our own world, we would be the best farmers we could be.

How to Sow

The way you sow is the thought you sow. Life is about planting seeds daily!

How deep are you planting yours? Do you plant them in everything you do? Do you always expect a harvest? Have you ever realized that sometimes the soil you sow in may not return a harvest?

I want to emphasize the attitude we keep is everything when we sow. How are you sowing at this very moment while holding this book, reading these words? Are you truly open toward sowing something, in order for you to get a harvest from this book?

The Power of Sowing
Remember, it's not as important in how much you sow, as it is the *way* you sow it!

Planting Light Seeds
Those are the ones you may think don't matter much, but they do. This is the daily routine of consciously spreading your light through the sowing of a smile, a gentle touch, a kind word, or a thoughtful gesture.

If you only understood what a smile could do…
For the rejected, the tired and all alone.
If only you knew what a kind gesture could do…
For the needy, the less fortunate, the poor.
If only, but you don't, probably because this…
Was never bestowed unto you!

Take the time to make your light shine, because…
If only you knew what a smile could do for you,
If only you knew what a kind gesture
could do for you…
It will surely be bestowed back unto you!

Don't forget our God does not return,
He multiplies our blessings…
So for every smile and every kind gesture you do…
Prepare to receive a heart filled with
joy and a guarantee that
Kindness from others is on its way to you.

Finale

I knew that I had made it to the end of this journey finally! No more waiting, no more thought processes, just the complete release for what it was intended to be—a book, a message written with love. It is meant to be both empowering and forgiving, and my hope is that you have been able to finish this read with both in your heart as well as in your mind.

You see, as I sit knowing that I have only a few hours before returning to my regular schedule of life, there is only one last thing I need to share with you:

My walk with God has been an ever-growing one.
My walk with God has been a forgiving one.
My walk with God has changed my heart!
My walk with God has taught me many things.
My walk with God has shown me that no matter where I am in life, no matter what I am going through, He knows that I am imperfect, but He loves me in any way that I come to Him!
My walk with God has given me the ultimate gift, that of the Spirit Walker.
My walk with God has given me an opportunity to ask you if you would like to become one too.

Big Decision, Baby Steps

Sometimes making a decision, any kind of decision, can be difficult. But when you make it one small step at a time, one fragment of moment at a time, progressing toward something new and away from something old is very achievable!

I have journeyed over the years in a way that has allowed me to do such a thing in my spiritual life, and I am here to say that it is absolutely awesome! Every time I tried to walk in the Spirit but failed to do so, it still brought me closer to God regardless, in one way or another. You see, God loves me no less because I am not succeeding or doing what it is that I think I should be doing to serve Him best—He loves me just the same for trying!

Saying Yes to God

It is a freedom that comes with a feeling, and there is nothing like it in this world. No drug, no gift, no trip can explain or can fill you like the gift of being *free in Christ*. It can be instilled in you at such a cellular level that your spiritual walk will be strengthened and brought to a whole new level.

What you need to know, and not understand, is that knowing what is yours and understanding what is yours are two different things.

When you know something, there is conviction and certainty. When you try to understand something, there can be confusion and doubt. What you need to believe is that you are being given an opportunity to live your heaven on earth and through the sacrifice of Jesus's death, you have been provided with power that is beyond any full human comprehension. God does not expect us to fully comprehend all that has and is transpiring on earth, nor does He expect us to fully grasp all that He has to offer us.

What he does expect us to do is hold on to something that He had to pay a very high price for. He wants us to know that there is a power that comes to us through praying. It is a calling in the presence of God Almighty Himself into our very spirit and the wonder of all that is available to us at all times.

Wherever You May Be

So wherever you may be right now, you can embrace this way of life, that of the Spirit Walker. It is a choice, I know, and I want to make sure before you go, if you so wish to make this choice, to simply repeat after me.

Dear Heavenly Father,
I believe that Jesus is your son
and that He died on the cross for me.
Please come into my life and change my heart
and also be Lord of my life.
Most importantly, wash me clean of my sins!
In Jesus's name, I pray and ask
Amen!

If you've just prayed this prayer and meant it wholeheartedly, I only have one thing to say to you: "Welcome to the family!"

Oh and by the way, just so you know, right now in heaven, there is a band of angels singing songs of praise because you now have a place to call home!

THE SOWERS TRUST
BACK COVER 2014

Because there are certain things you just never want to go through in your lifetime, let alone write about them in an open book, I chose to do so because I want you to understand the depth of the pit I was in and how God's mercy and grace lifted me out of it.

There are some things that when I stop and think about them I realize how hurtful, painful, and devastating they were to go through. This I would never wish on anyone, but this is exactly what I had to go through to survive.

Then one day I had decided I had enough of doing this on my own, so I took a knee and prayed and asked God with a wrench-filled heart to take over my life—and He did.

This is about a journey I—and so many countless others—took post-2008, after the great demise of the real estate market crash of 2008. To this day, many are still reeling from the effects of this terrible historic time. Some were forced to walk down paths to places where they never thought they would find themselves, let alone survive there. Many people could not face what lay ahead of them and hundreds of thousands more lives were changed forever.

*The Sower's **TRUST** is about my spiritual growth and journey during these times, and although Satan's intent was to keep me silent, God used it all to help me grow His kingdom.*

Carol Woolgar resides in Central, Florida with her two boys, Zachary and Bradley

www.ingramcontent.com/pod-product-compliance
Lightning Source LLC
LaVergne TN
LVHW020423080526
838202LV00055B/5021